From the desk of:
Ms. Harrison

Bugs That Kill

Gary Raham

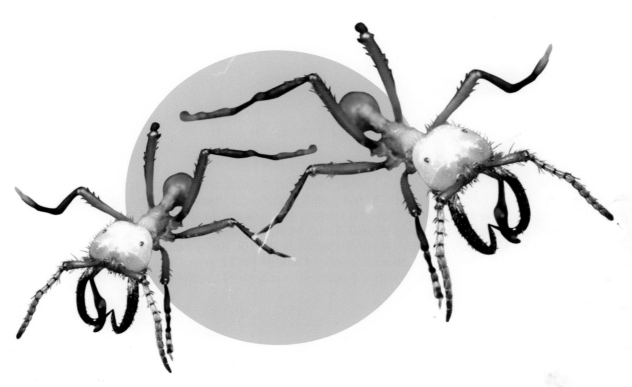

Marshall Cavendish
Benchmark

New York

Marshall Cavendish Benchmark
99 White Plains Road
Tarrytown, NY 10591
www.marshallcavendish.us

Library of Congress Cataloging-in-Publication Data
Raham, Gary.
    Bugs that kill / by Gary Raham.
    p. cm. -- (Bug alert)
    Includes bibliographical references and index.
    ISBN 978-0-7614-3185-5
1. Insects--Juvenile literature. I. Title.
    QL467.2.R34 2009
    595.7--dc22
    2008014831

The photographs in this book are used by permission and through the courtesy of:

Half Title : Dr. Morley Read/ Shutterstock
Joseph Calev/ Shutterstock: 4tr, Harold Taylor/ Oxford Scientific/ Photolibrary: 4b, spad/ Istockphoto: 5, arlindo71/
Istockphoto: 6tr, Howard Grill/ Shutterstock: 7, Meul / ARCO/ Naturepl: 9, Hway Kiong Lim/ Shutterstock: 11, Mark
Kostich/ Istockphoto: 12tr, Gregory MD./ Photo Researchers/ Photolibrary: 13, John Bell/ Shutterstock: 14tr, DAVID
M DENNIS/ Animals Animals/ Photolibrary: 15, Maik Dobiey/Photographersdirect: 17, TornPicture Photo Restoration/
18tr, Robert Shantz / Alamy: 19, Dr. Morley Read/ Shutterstock: 20tr, Dr. Morley Read/ Shutterstock: 21, Jim Jurica/
Istockphoto: 22tr, Satoshi Kuribayashi/ Oxford Scientific/ Photolibrary: 23, Zeno/ Istockphoto: 24tr, Antagain/
Istockphoto: 25, Vnlit/ Istockphoto: 26tr, Nature Production/ Naturepl: 27, Jason Ng/ Shutterstock: 28tr, Andy
Sands/ Naturepl: 29.

Cover photo: Bill Beatty/ Photolibrary

Illustrations : Q2A Media Art bank.

Illustrators: Indranil Ganguly, Rishi Bhardwaj, Kusum Kala, Pooja Shukla

Created by: Q2A Media

Creative Director: Simmi Sikka

Series Editor: Maura Christopher

Series Art Director: Sudakshina Basu

Series Designers: Mansi Mittal, Rati Mathur and Shruti Bahl

Photo research by Anju Pathak

Series Project Managers: Ravneet Kaur and Shekhar Kapur

Printed in Malaysia

135642

Contents

A Bug Eat Bug World

Bugs may seem scary because they look weird and seem to creep and crawl on a million legs. These invertebrates (animals without backbones) are just trying to eat, grow up, and raise families. In the process, they may kill each other. Sometimes, they kill humans by mistake.

Scientists call six-legged bugs *insects*. Insects have three body parts, jaws called mandibles, and **antennae** for smelling and touching the world around them. Eight-legged bugs called **arachnids** include spiders, scorpions, ticks, and their relatives. Arachnids' bodies are made up of two parts. They often use **fangs** and **stingers** to inject poison into their prey.

Bugs rule on planet Earth. Insects alone outnumber all other animals and plants combined. Bugs bristle with hairs that help them feel their world. No wonder that when bugs scoot, crawl, hop, buzz, bite, sting, and fly all over the place, people get "bugged." But bugs help recycle dead things. They **pollinate** plants and serve as food for other animals in nature's web of life.

▲ The head end of this beast has two arching antennae and fangs. A pair of legs at its tail end serve nicely as pinchers.

Awesome Arthropods

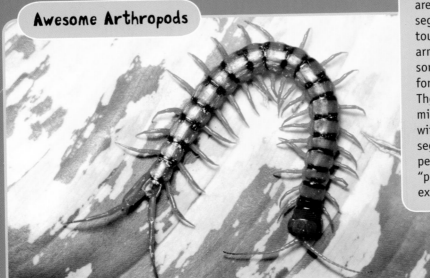

Segments and Body Armor

Both insects and arachnids are kinds of **arthropods**, segmented animals with tough outer shells like body armor. Arthropods of various sorts have lived in oceans for over 500 million years. They came ashore nearly 400 million years ago. Centipedes with twenty or more body segments and two legs per segment make handsome "poster bugs"—the best examples of arthropods.

Males with big mandibles often fight each other for females.

The head segment supports mouthparts and sense organs.

Legs attach to the middle body segment.

Beetles have six strong, jointed walking legs.

Beetles fold flying wings beneath hard, protective wings.

Find the three body segments, six legs, and two antennae on this stag beetle. This insect has jaws so big that they look like antlers!

Armed for Offense

Insects tend to take the snatch-and-chew or the stab-and-suck approach to attacking other animals or defending themselves. Beetles grab prey with big jaws. Robber flies stab and paralyze other flying insects and suck out their insides.

Spiders use fangs to bite their prey and inject chemicals that begin to **predigest** their victim. When the victim's insides are goopy enough, they bring the victim to their mouth with armlike **pedipalps**. They mash their prey with strong jaws and squeeze out every tasty drop. Spiders and some centipedes create **silk** in special **glands** to trap prey, wrap it up, or build nests and egg cases.

Scorpions and their close relatives use pinchers to grab prey. Scorpions, bees, and wasps come equipped with stingers for offense and defense. The poison they inject with stingers and fangs sometimes causes severe reactions.

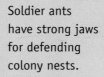

▶
Soldier ants have strong jaws for defending colony nests.

As Fast as the Wind

Wind scorpions are arachnids that do not have pinchers or stingers. But they crush prey to death with their enormous jaws. They eat mostly other bugs but can kill small lizards. They run as fast as the wind on three pairs of legs. They sense **vibrations** with **organs** beneath their fourth pair of legs. At home in dry climates, they hunt mostly during the day.

Jaws with Legs

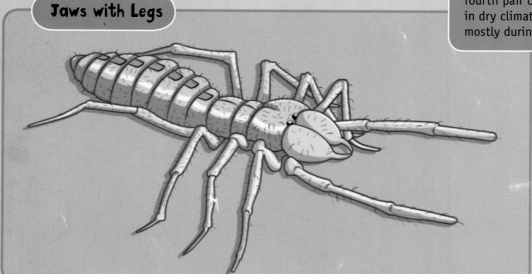

When a bug's colors match its favorite plant, it's hard to see it hiding there.

This spider's fangs have latched on tight. It is almost time to suck up lunch.

A crab spider's long front legs open wide for a dangerous "bug hug."

Crab spiders pretend to be flower parts and attack visiting bugs.

Centipedes

All centipedes kill other bugs for food by using fangs that inject poison. Some centipedes have been fooled into biting glass beads dipped in fly guts. Obviously, they can taste and touch better than they can see.

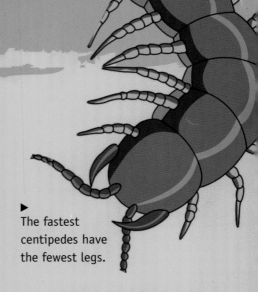

▶ The fastest centipedes have the fewest legs.

What Are They?

Centipedes are primitive arthropods with long bodies made up of many similar segments. Each segment has a pair of legs. They live in leaf litter, in soil, under bark, and sometimes in people's houses. Their bite usually does not hurt humans, but it may sting.

Buggy Body Odor

Most centipedes hunt at night. Like insects, they are bugs with antennae, but like spiders, they may also produce some silk for capturing their prey. They may defend themselves by throwing sticky gunk at enemies with their last pair of legs or making stinky chemicals other bugs do not like.

Life Cycle

1. When a male centipede finds a female, they touch antennae. The male follows the female.
2. Male centipedes weave small silk webs and deposit a packet of sperm that the female then picks up to **fertilize** her eggs.
3. The female lays her eggs and, in some species, may lick them.
4. Some centipede females also coil around their eggs and protect them until they hatch.

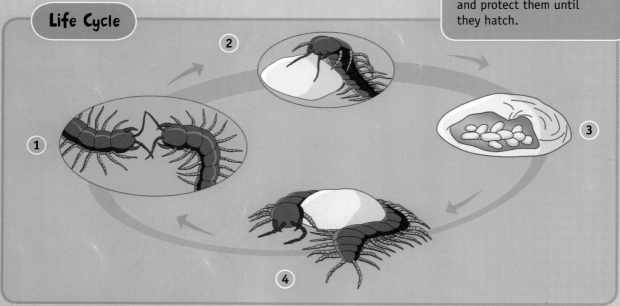

Life Cycle

Centipede antennae are organs of taste and touch.

Centipede fangs can cause a nasty sting.

How many pairs of walking legs does this centipede have?

Body segments hook together for fast running.

Although *centi* means "one hundred" and *pes* means "foot," centipedes usually have fewer than one hundred legs.

The last pair of legs make great pinchers.

Jumping Killers

Jumping spiders hunt like cats, stalking **their prey and then pouncing. Their two huge front eyes look like goggles. They use their six smaller eyes to watch out for things next to and behind them.**

What Are They?

Although jumping spiders are spiders, they do not make webs to catch insects. Instead, they stick a **dragline** of silk behind them when they hunt. If they jump off a leaf and miss their target, they can haul themselves back again! Jumpers make silk nests where they lay eggs, **molt** (shed their old skins), and rest.

Dance for Your Life, Daddy

Males must wave their front legs, twitch, shake, and do a special zigzag dance before they can mate with a female. Otherwise, they get eaten.

▲ Jumpers eat mosquitoes and other bugs that are pests to people.

Life Cycle

1. A female jumping spider builds a silk case on a leaf or branch or in cracks on the sides of buildings.
2. She lays her eggs inside the case and guards them until they hatch.
3. Baby spiders emerge, looking like tiny adults. They spread out to hunt on their own.
4. As they grow, the baby spiders shed their skin.

Life Cycle

Two large eyes in front form clear, cameralike images of prey.

Six small eyes detect motion and possible danger.

This jumper's green fangs inject poison.

Spiders have eight walking legs. Among them, pedipalps (just in front of the fangs) handle prey.

A jumper uses its third or fourth pair of legs for jumping. Some species can jump twenty-five times their body length. The jumper uses its first pair of legs for waving at other jumpers.

Widows and Recluses

The venom of black widow and brown recluse spiders is dangerous to humans and their pets. Widows spin ragged webs near houses. A red hourglass spot on their black, shiny belly makes them easy to spot. Brown recluses have a violin-shaped mark on their backs. They often live under houses.

What Are They?

Widows are cobweb-weaving spiders. Special combs on their feet help them walk on their webs. They hang belly up in their webs, hourglass mark showing. Brown recluse spiders use sticky silk to trap prey. Both spiders are shy. Don't bug them and they won't bite.

Nasty Poisons

Black widow spiders inject poison fifteen times more powerful than rattlesnake venom. The venom from brown recluses can kill skin around the bite and cause a wound that heals slowly and may leave a large scar. Look carefully before reaching into dark, cobwebby corners and woodpiles.

▲ The widows you see are all females. Males are tiny and may get eaten.

Spider bite symptoms
From a black widow spider: People feel extreme pain within ten to sixty minutes of being bitten. They may get dizzy and want to throw up. Belly muscles become as hard as a board, eyes water, and jaw muscles tighten. **Antivenin** to counteract the toxin and other medical treatments can reduce the symptoms quickly.
From a brown recluse spider: The poisonous venom from this spider kills skin near the bite and may cause a large wound that is slow to heal. The poison damages blood cells, which can lead to kidney failure.

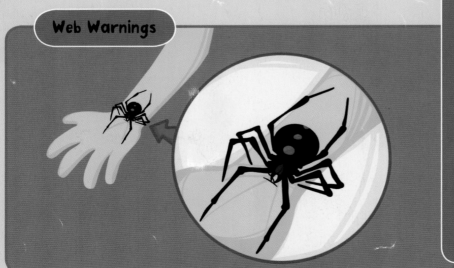

Web Warnings

Male recluses may have small **abdomens**. A female's abdomen may swell with eggs.

Both recluses and widows have long legs.

Male spiders use their pedipalps to fertilize a female's eggs with sperm.

This big abdomen belongs to a female.

Scorpions

Most of the 1,200 or so kinds of scorpions live in warm, dry places like deserts. They range in size from 4/10 of an inch to 7 inches (10 to 180 millimeters) long. They use big pinchers to grab their prey.

What Are They?

Scorpions are a type of arachnid. Sometimes they use stingers on the end of their tails to quiet their prey before they eat them. The stingers also discourage animals that prey on scorpions. The venom injected with the stingers of a few scorpions can be painful or even cause death in humans.

▲ This scorpion is ready to strike.

Scorpion Family History

Scorpions may have been some of the earliest land-living arthropods. The oldest known eight-legged bug was a scorpion that lived 400 million years ago. In the oceans 390 million years ago, scorpion relatives called eurypterids sometimes grew to be 8 feet (2.4 meters) long!

Life Cycle

1. Fertilized eggs develop inside the female.
2. Tiny scorpions hatch inside the female scorpion and crawl out.
3. The tiny scorpions scramble up onto the female's back, sometimes using her pincher legs as ramps.
4. The young ride on the female for a while and molt several times before becoming old enough to hunt on their own.

Life Cycle

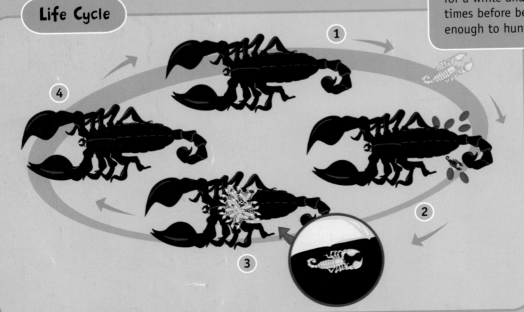

Burrowing scorpions hold their tails straight up.

The stinger curls under the tail.

Scorpions have two eyes in front and two to five eyes on either side of their head.

Males have bigger pinchers and longer tails than females.

Scorpions have four pair of walking legs like other arachnids.

Scorpions glow at night when exposed to ultraviolet light—a good way to find them in the desert.

Hunters and Wanderers

Some spiders actively hunt prey, but don't use a web. Common wolf spiders wait in fields, under rocks, and in burrows for other bugs to bump into them. Tropical wandering spiders such as the Brazilian wandering spider may be both aggressive **and dangerous to humans.**

▲ Male wolf spiders wave their hairy pedipalps to attract mates.

What Are They?

Wolf and wandering spiders are two related groups of spiders. Neither makes webs but may dig tunnels and burrows and line them with silk. Wolf spiders use their good eyesight and sense of touch to hunt. Many species are active during the day.

A Tropical Wandering Spider

Unlike most shy spiders, Brazilian wandering spiders can be aggressive. Their bites are painful. People who are bitten break into a sweat and feel cold and tense. Their heart rate also speeds up. Wandering spiders sometimes hitch rides on bananas shipped from South America.

Wolf Spider Life Cycle

1. Females spin a silk cocoon in which they lay eggs. Unlike many spiders, they keep this egg case attached to their silk-making organs, the spinnerets.
2. When as many as a hundred young hatch, they crawl up on the female's back.
3. After about a week, the young spiders leave to hunt on their own.

Life Cycle

Wandering spiders have two or three claws at the tip of each leg.

Wandering spiders raise their long first pair of legs when threatened.

Wandering spiders often have dark stripes on their backs.

Wolf and wandering spiders have better eyesight than web-weaving spiders.

Hunting Wasps

Hunting wasps do not kill their prey right away. Instead, they lay their eggs in or on the prey animal. Young wasp larvae **eat their prey** host **from the outside in or the inside out.**

What Are They?

Wasps are insects, so they have six legs, a head, a thorax (to which the legs are attached), and an abdomen. In wasps, a thin waist connects the thorax to the abdomen. Hunting wasps such as the tarantula hawk use their stinger to paralyze prey.

Choosy Eaters

Often a particular kind of wasp only eats one kind of bug. Some wasps hunt only beetles, crickets, bees, flies, spiders, or even other wasps. The tarantula hawk wasp hunts large, hairy tarantulas.

▲ This wasp has its stinger ready for action.

Tarantula Hawk Wasp Life Cycle

1. A female hunts for a tarantula and paralyzes it with a sting.
2. It then drags the spider to a burrow and lays an egg on it.
3. The egg hatches into a wormlike larva that grows as it eats the still-living spider.
4. When the larva has eaten enough, it enters a resting stage called a **pupa**.
5. Eventually an adult wasp emerges from the pupa.

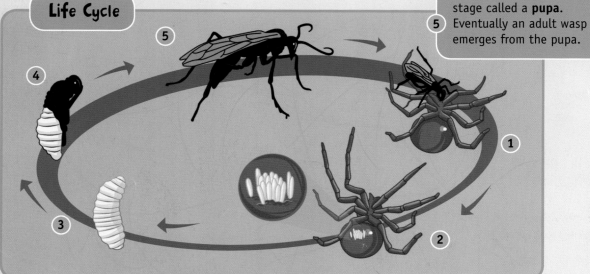

Life Cycle

Female wasps have curved antennae, and males have straight ones.

Tarantulas are often bitten on the belly when they rear back to show their fangs.

Wasps remember landmarks such as sticks and pebbles to find their way back to the nest.

Tarantula hawk wasps have large, blue-black bodies and orange wings.

Driver Ants

Driver ants in Africa and legionary ants in South America hunt in swarms of up to 20 million workers. Worker ants flow out from the nest in such huge numbers that they look like streams of black water.

A worker ant tends a young larva.

What Are They?

Ants are social insects that live in **colonies**. Different colony members are built for different jobs. A driver ant queen can grow to be 2 inches (5 centimeters) long. Worker ants are much smaller. Soldier ants bite prey and potential enemies with huge jaws.

Vicious But Not Too Smart

Driver ants will swarm and bite to death small or wounded animals that cannot get out of their way. On a flat, clean surface, however, the ants can become confused and move around in a circle until they die.

Driver Ant Life Cycle

1. The single queen in a colony lays eggs that are tended by workers.
2. Larvae hatch from the eggs. Workers also feed the young larvae.
3. The larvae spin cocoons for themselves. Inside the cocoons, the larvae change into adults.
4. Adult ants emerge from the cocoons. They are all worker and soldier ants. Potential queens must be fed a special diet to become queens.

Life Cycle

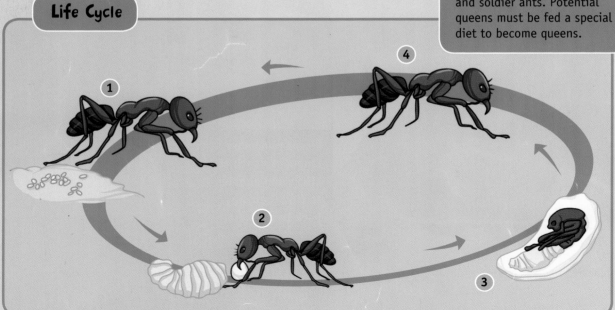

Army ants march on sturdy legs.

Ants use antennae to touch and smell.

Soldier driver ants sport hefty jaws.

Like other insects, ants have three body parts and six legs for walking.

A Beetle's World

One of every three insects is a beetle. In fact, one of every four animals is a beetle. In both their larval and adult forms, tiger beetles prey on other bugs. They look a bit like six-legged tanks with big jaws.

What Are They?

Tiger beetles have bulging eyes and black or brown spotted bodies. A set of hard outer wings close over thin flying wings like a pair of folding doors. Adults may pounce on their prey like a cat. Tiger beetle larvae wait at the top of burrows and grab moving prey.

▲ Some tiger beetles shine with metallic blues and greens.

Hard to Catch

Tiger beetles live in sandy, open areas such as beaches and dry riverbeds. Unlike most other beetles, tiger beetles fly well and move quickly on long legs. They are not easy to catch by hand. Most collectors use an insect net.

Life Cycle

1 Females lay small, oval, cream-colored eggs one at a time in the soil.
2 The egg develops into an S-shaped larva in the soil, usually under rocks or old boards. The larva hunts from a burrow.
3 A larva may spend a winter in the soil or develop into a pupa first.
4 Adults emerge from the pupa and move aboveground.

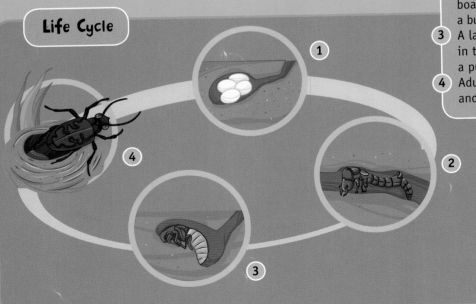

Life Cycle

Big, buggy **compound eyes** see movement easily.

Threadlike antennae emerge from just below the eyes.

Fingerlike jaw parts help handle food.

Huge jaws make short work of nabbing prey.

Praying Mantises

A praying mantis, a kind of mantid, often sits very still. It tucks its large forelegs beneath its triangular head as if it were praying. Mantids often look like a leaf, stick, or flower to fool other bugs. When prey comes too close, the forelegs dart out as fast as a heartbeat to snatch a meal.

"Who me? ▶
I'm just a twig."

What Are They?
Mantids are insects with great vision and long forelegs for grabbing prey. Most mantids are usually more than 1 inch (2.5 centimeters) long, with skinny bodies. Males are smaller than females.

How Males Keep Their Heads (or Not)
Male mantids must approach females carefully, staying away from their nasty forelegs. Sometimes the female grabs the male's head while mating and begins to eat him, head first. The male may lose his head, but the female gets a good meal before laying her eggs.

Life Cycle

1. Mantids lay from 30 to 300 eggs in papery cases, usually on twigs and weeds. Eggs spend winter in the case before hatching.
2. Young mantids quickly separate. Otherwise, they tend to eat one another.
3. Females release chemicals that attract males. After mating, males escape their mates most of the time to breed again.
4. Females lay their eggs in bubbly foam that eventually hardens into the case that will survive the winter.

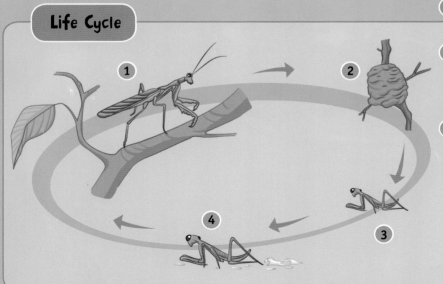

Life Cycle

24

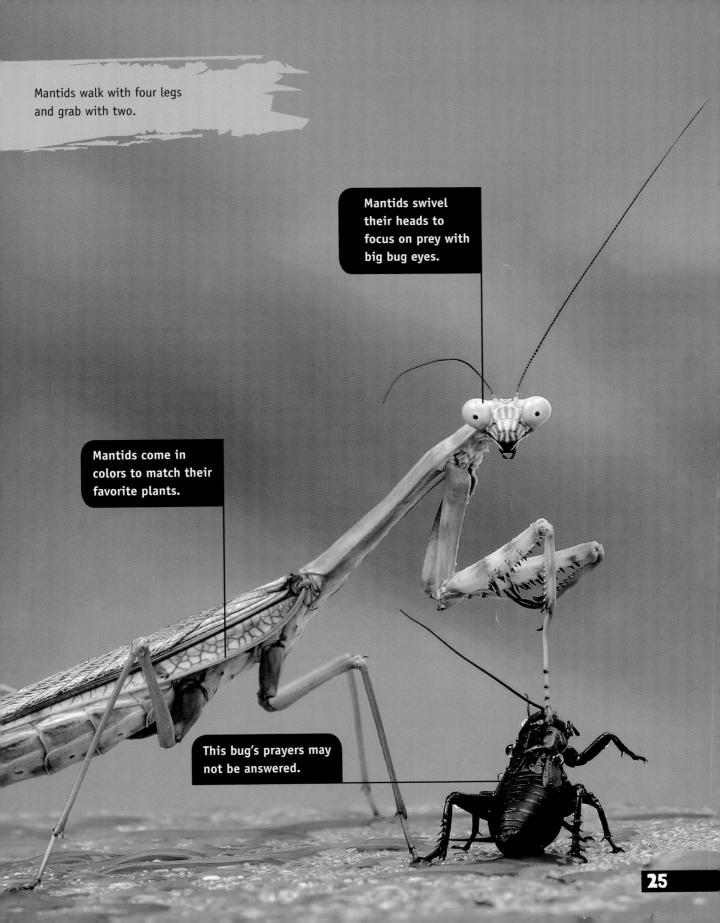

Mantids walk with four legs and grab with two.

Mantids swivel their heads to focus on prey with big bug eyes.

Mantids come in colors to match their favorite plants.

This bug's prayers may not be answered.

Flying Dragons

Dragonfly adults look like tiny, two-winged airplanes. They can dart and hover like helicopters. They use their huge eyes to spot other flying insects and scoop them up into legs held like an open basket.

What Are They?

Dragonflies are primitive insects that eat many mosquitoes, flies, and other flying insects. They spend most of their lives as **nymphs** in fresh water, where they breathe with gills. Modern dragonflies have wingspans up to 7.5 inches (19 cm). One **fossil** dragonfly's wingspan measured 28 inches (71 cm).

▲ Why are dragonflies sometimes called "Mosquito Hawks"?

Aquatic Hunters

A dragonfly nymph holds a masklike **mouthpart** over its face with a long, foldable arm. When its prey comes close, the arm snaps out. A claw on the end of the mask hooks the meal and brings it to the nymph's jaws. To move quickly, nymphs squirt water out of their rear ends.

Life Cycle

1. Females lay eggs in the water.
2. The eggs hatch into nymphs.
3. Nymphs may live for five or six years before crawling out of the water onto a plant and molting into an adult.

Life Cycle

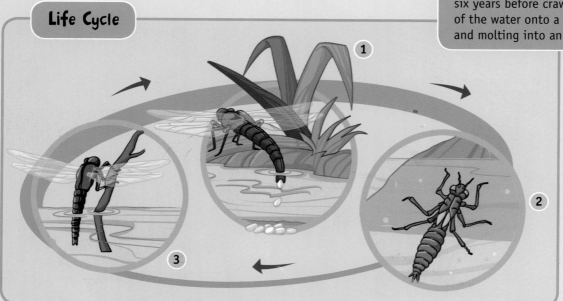

Vein patterns in dragon fly wings differ from species to species.

Basket anyone? Use your legs like a dragonfly.

This bee will soon be in a dragonfly belly.

Adult dragonfly eyes provide wraparound vision.

Robber Flies

Robber flies zoom upward from their perch on a tall plant and stab other flying insects with their knifelike mouthparts. The robbers return to their perch, suck the insides out of their prey, and drop the remains on the ground.

► Stout, bristly legs are helpful for catching and holding struggling prey.

What Are They?

Robber flies, insects in the fly family, often look like bees or wasps. Unlike these other insects, however, robber flies sit still on plants for long periods of time until a likely victim passes by. They have two huge eyes (and three tiny ones) protected by hairs that resemble a mustache.

Fooling a Robber Fly

Robber flies watch over territory up to 5 yards from their base plant. Because their eyes respond to movement so accurately, they sometimes will try to attack a small pebble or other object thrown within 3 feet or so of their perch.

Life Cycle

1. Male robber flies often bring a food treat to females when they come courting. This helps to ensure that the females don't attack and eat them.
2. Females lay their eggs in the soil or, less frequently, on plants.
3. The eggs hatch into young fly larvae, which spend the winter in the soil. Eventually the larvae change into a resting stage, or pupae.
4. When the weather warms, the pupa hatches into an adult fly. Many details of the robber flies' life cycle are still unknown.

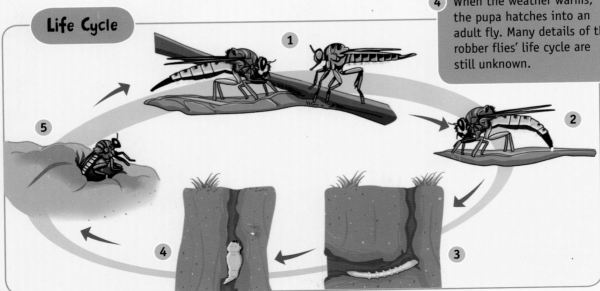

Life Cycle

1
2
3
4
5

Robber flies have large eyes to focus on their prey.

Heavy muscles in a robber fly's thorax help make it a strong flyer.

A mustache of bristles protects robber flies' eyes when they stab prey with their knifelike mouthparts.

Although robber flies look like bees, they have no stingers.

Bugs Data

Books

Birch, Robin. *Spiders Up Close* (Minibeasts Up Close). Chicago: Raintree, 2004.

Elder, Vanessa, Carolyn Jackson, Monique Peterson, and Gary Raham. *Insects* (Discovery Channel Books). Pleasantville, NY: Gareth Stevens Publishing, 2002.

Hartley, Karen, Philip Taylor, and Chris MacRo. *Centipede* (Bug Books). Chicago: Heinemann, 2006.

O'Neill, Amanda. *Insects and Bugs* (Curious Kids Guides). London: Kingfisher Publications, 2002.

Parker, Edward. *Insects and Spiders*. Chicago: Raintree, 2002.

Internet Sites

Visit these Web sites for more information:

Insectarium: An All Bug Museum
http://www.insectarium.com/insectarium.htm

National Geographic: Bees and Wasps
http://video.nationalgeographic.com/video/player/animals/bugs-animals/bees-and-wasps/wasp_paper_nest.html

National Geographic: Jumping Spiders
http://video.nationalgeographic.com/video/player/kids/animals-pets-kids/bugs-kids/jumping-spider-kids.html

Glossary

abdomen: The region of the body that is farthest back in insects and arachnids.

aggressive: Forceful, ready to attack.

antenna (plural: antennae): A feeler located on the head of insects and other bugs.

antivenin: A chemical that stops a poison from working.

arachnid: Invertebrates with eight legs, such as spiders, ticks, and mites.

arthropods: Animals with a body divided into segments, a tough outer shell, and jointed limbs.

colony: A group of animals, such as ants or honeybees, that live and work together.

compound eyes: Eyes made up of many separate lenses.

dragline: Anchor thread of silk used by jumping spiders.

fangs: Curved, hollow mouthparts for injecting venom.

fertilize: To make able to produce eggs.

fossil: The remains of an ancient plant or animal preserved in rock.

glands: Parts of the body that make important chemicals.

host: A living animal that serves as food and shelter for another creature.

larva (plural: larvae): The wormlike immature form of an insect.

molt: To shed skin to grow into an adult form. Most bugs molt.

mouthpart: Body part near the mouth used for gathering or eating food.

nymph: A wingless, immature stage in some insects.

organs: Parts of the body specialized to do certain jobs.

paralyze: To block the action of muscles so that animals cannot move.

pedipalps: A pair of feelers between a spider's front legs.

pollinate: To transfer pollen from flower to flower so that the plant can grow seeds and create new plants.

predigest: To begin to break down food with chemicals outside the stomach.

pupa (plural: pupae): A cocoonlike resting stage of an insect just before adulthood.

silk: A sticky white material made by spiders and some other bugs that can be drawn out in a long thread.

stalk: To follow without being seen.

stinger: A body part that can puncture an animal and inject poison.

venom: Poison that usually acts on an animal's nervous system.

vibrations: Tiny movements back and forth or up and down.

Index